Contents

Robert Louis Stevenson's

A Child's Garden of Verses

Illustrated by
Susan Bonners

GOLDEN PRESS • NEW YORK
Western Publishing Company, Inc.
Racine, Wisconsin

To Any Reader

As from the house your mother sees
You playing round the garden trees,
So you may see, if you will look
Through the windows of this book,
Another child, far, far away,
And in another garden, play.
But do not think you can at all,
By knocking on the window, call
That child to hear you. He intent
Is all on his play-business bent.
He does not hear; he will not look,
Nor yet be lured out of this book.
For, long ago, the truth to say,
He has grown up and gone away,
And it is but a child of air
That lingers in the garden there.

The Swing

How do you like to go up in a swing,
    Up in the air so blue?
Oh, I do think it the pleasantest thing
    Ever a child can do!

Up in the air and over the wall,
    Till I can see so wide,
Rivers and trees and cattle and all
    Over the countryside—

Till I look down on the garden green,
    Down on the roof so brown—
Up in the air I go flying again,
    Up in the air and down!

Foreign Lands

Up into the cherry tree
Who should climb but little me!
I held the trunk with both my hands
And looked abroad on foreign lands.

I saw the next-door garden lie,
Adorned with flowers, before my eye,
And many pleasant places more
That I had never seen before.

I saw the dimpling river pass
And be the sky's blue looking glass;
The dusty roads go up and down
With people tramping into town.

If I could find a higher tree
Farther and farther I should see,
To where the grown-up river slips
Into the sea among the ships,

To where the roads on either hand
Lead onward into fairyland,
Where all the children dine at five,
And all the playthings come alive.

9

My Ship and I

O it's I that am the captain of a tidy little ship,
  Of a ship that goes a-sailing on the pond;
And my ship it keeps a-turning all around and all about;
But when I'm a little older, I shall find the secret out
  How to send my vessel sailing on beyond.

For I mean to grow as little as the dolly at the helm,
  And the dolly I intend to come alive;
And with him beside to help me, it's a-sailing I shall go,
It's a-sailing on the water, when the jolly breezes blow
  And the vessel goes a divie-divie-dive.

O it's then you'll see me sailing through the rushes and the reeds,
   And you'll hear the water singing at the prow;
For beside the dolly sailor, I'm to voyage and explore,
To land upon the island where no dolly was before,
   And to fire the penny cannon in the bow.

11

Where Go the Boats?

Dark brown is the river,
    Golden is the sand.
It flows along forever,
    With trees on either hand.

Green leaves a-floating,
    Castles of the foam,
Boats of mine a-boating—
    Where will all come home?

On goes the river
      And out past the mill,
Away down the valley,
      Away down the hill.

Away down the river,
      A hundred miles or more,
Other little children
      Shall bring my boats ashore.

13

Bed in Summer

In winter I get up at night
And dress by yellow candlelight.
In summer, quite the other way,
I have to go to bed by day.

I have to go to bed and see
The birds still hopping on the tree,
Or hear the grown-up people's feet
Still going past me in the street.

And does it not seem hard to you,
When all the sky is clear and blue,
And I should like so much to play,
To have to go to bed by day?

15

My Shadow

I have a little shadow that goes in and out with me,
And what can be the use of him is more than I can see.
He is very, very like me from the heels up to the head;
And I see him jump before me, when I jump into my bed.

The funniest thing about him is the way he likes to grow—
Not at all like proper children, which is always very slow;
For he sometimes shoots up taller like an india-rubber ball,
And he sometimes gets so little that there's none of him at all.

He hasn't got a notion of how children ought to play,
And can only make a fool of me in every sort of way.
He stays so close beside me, he's a coward you can see;
I'd think shame to stick to nursie as that shadow sticks to me!

One morning, very early, before the sun was up,
I rose and found the shining dew on every buttercup;
But my lazy little shadow, like an arrant sleepyhead,
Had stayed at home behind me and was fast asleep in bed.

Block City

What are you able to build with your blocks?
Castles and palaces, temples and docks.
Rain may keep raining, and others go roam,
But I can be happy and building at home.

Let the sofa be mountains, the carpet be sea,
There I'll establish a city for me:
A kirk and a mill and a palace beside,
And a harbor as well where my vessels may ride.

Great is the palace with pillar and wall,
A sort of a tower on the top of it all,
And steps coming down in an orderly way
To where my toy vessels lie safe in the bay.

18

This one is sailing and that one is moored:
Hark to the song of the sailors on board!
And see, on the steps of my palace, the kings
Coming and going with presents and things!

Now I have done with it, down let it go!
All in a moment the town is laid low.
Block upon block lying scattered and free,
What is there left of my town by the sea?

Yet as I saw it, I see it again,
The kirk and the palace, the ships and the men,
And as long as I live and where'er I may be,
I'll always remember my town by the sea.

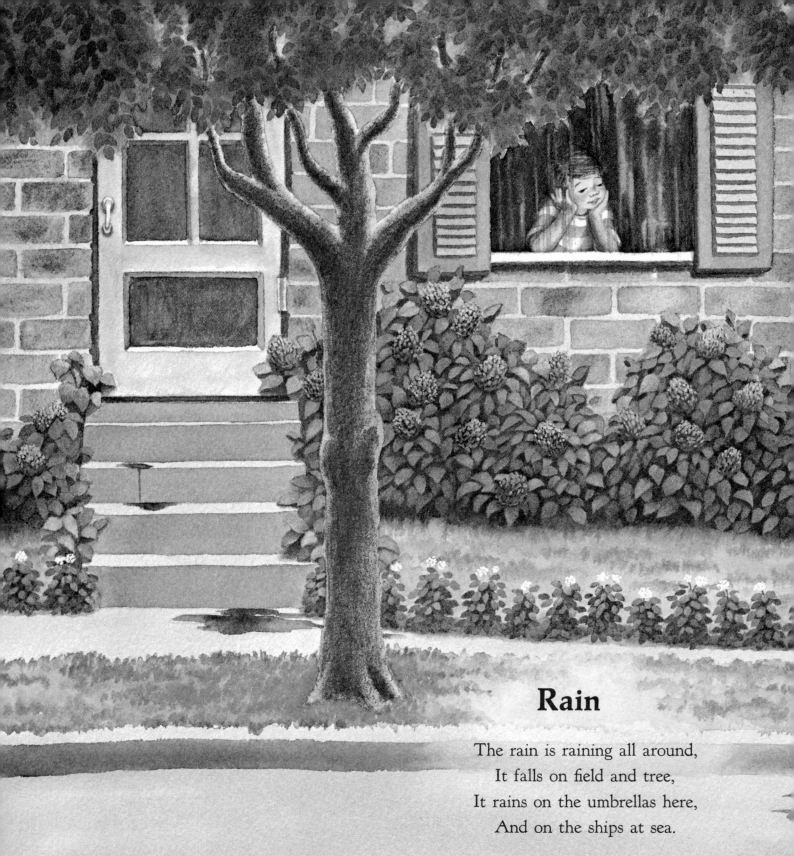

Rain

The rain is raining all around,
It falls on field and tree,
It rains on the umbrellas here,
And on the ships at sea.

The Flowers

All the names I know from nurse:
Gardener's garters, Shepherd's purse,
Bachelor's buttons, Lady's smock,
And the Lady Hollyhock.

Fairy places, fairy things,
Fairy woods where the wild bee wings,
Tiny trees for tiny dames—
These must all be fairy names!

Tiny woods below whose boughs
Shady fairies weave a house;
Tiny treetops, rose or thyme,
Where the braver fairies climb!

Fair are grown-up people's trees,
But the fairest woods are these;
Where, if I were not so tall,
I should live for good and all.

23

The Hayloft

Through all the pleasant meadow side
    The grass grew shoulder-high,
Till the shining scythes went far and wide
    And cut it down to dry.

Those green and sweetly smelling crops
    They led in wagons home;
And they piled them here in mountain tops
    For mountaineers to roam.

Here is Mount Clear, Mount Rusty-Nail,
  Mount Eagle and Mount High;
The mice that in these mountains dwell,
  No happier are than I!

Oh, what a joy to clamber there,
  Oh, what a place for play,
With the sweet, the dim, the dusty air,
  The happy hills of hay!

Farewell to the Farm

The coach is at the door at last;
The eager children, mounting fast
And kissing hands, in chorus sing:
Good-bye, good-bye, to everything!

To house and garden, field and lawn,
The meadow gates we swang upon,
To pump and stable, tree and swing,
Good-bye, good-bye, to everything!

And fare you well for evermore,
O ladder at the hayloft door,
O hayloft where the cobwebs cling,
Good-bye, good-bye, to everything!

Crack goes the whip, and off we go;
The trees and houses smaller grow;
Last, round the woody turn we swing:
Good-bye, good-bye, to everything!

Autumn Fires

In the other gardens
　　And all up the vale,
From the autumn bonfires
　　See the smoke trail!

Pleasant summer over
　　And all the summer flowers,
The red fire blazes,
　　The gray smoke towers.

Sing a song of seasons!
　　Something bright in all!
Flowers in the summer,
　　Fires in the fall!

Windy Nights

Whenever the moon and stars are set,
   Whenever the wind is high,
All night long in the dark and wet,
   A man goes riding by.
Late in the night when the fires are out,
Why does he gallop and gallop about?

Whenever the trees are crying aloud,
   And ships are tossed at sea,
By, on the highway, low and loud,
   By at the gallop goes he.
By at the gallop he goes, and then
By he comes back at the gallop again.

Wintertime

Late lies the wintry sun abed,
A frosty, fiery sleepyhead;
Blinks but an hour or two; and then,
A blood-red orange, sets again.

Before the stars have left the skies,
At morning in the dark I rise;
And shivering in my nakedness,
By the cold candle, bathe and dress.

Close by the jolly fire I sit
To warm my frozen bones a bit;
Or with a reindeer-sled, explore
The colder countries round the door.

When to go out, my nurse doth wrap
Me in my comforter and cap;
The cold wind burns my face, and blows
Its frosty pepper up my nose.

Black are my steps on silver sod;
Thick blows my frosty breath abroad;
And tree and house, and hill and lake,
Are frosted like a wedding cake.

Picture Books in Winter

Summer fading, winter comes—
Frosty mornings, tingling thumbs,
Window robins, winter rooks,
And the picture storybooks.

Water now is turned to stone
Nurse and I can walk upon;
Still we find the flowing brooks
In the picture storybooks.

All the pretty things put by,
Wait upon the children's eye,
Sheep and shepherd's trees and crooks,
In the picture storybooks.

We may see how all things are,
Seas and cities, near and far,
And the flying fairies' looks,
In the picture storybooks.

How am I to sing your praise,
Happy chimney-corner days,
Sitting safe in nursery nooks,
Reading picture storybooks?

The Land of Counterpane

When I was sick and lay abed,
I had two pillows at my head,
And all my toys beside me lay
To keep me happy all the day.

And sometimes for an hour or so
I watched my leaden soldiers go,
With different uniforms and drills,
Among the bedclothes, through the hills;

And sometimes sent my ships in fleets
All up and down among the sheets;
Or brought my trees and houses out,
And planted cities all about.

I was the giant great and still
That sits upon the pillow-hill,
And sees before him, dale and plain,
The pleasant land of counterpane.

The Land of Nod

From breakfast on through all the day
At home among my friends I stay,
But every night I go abroad
Afar into the land of Nod.

All by myself I have to go,
With none to tell me what to do—
All alone beside the streams
And up the mountainsides of dreams.

The strangest things are there for me,
Both things to eat and things to see,
And many frightening sights abroad
Till morning in the land of Nod.

Try as I like to find the way,
I never can get back by day,
Nor can remember plain and clear
The curious music that I hear.

Nest Eggs

Birds all the sunny day
    Flutter and quarrel
Here in the arborlike
    Tent of the laurel.

Here in the fork
    The brown nest is seated;
Four little blue eggs
    The mother keeps heated.

While we stand watching her
   Staring like gabies,
Safe in each egg are the
   Bird's little babies.

Soon the frail eggs they shall
   Chip, and upspringing
Make all the April woods
   Merry with singing.

Younger than we are,
   O children, and frailer,
Soon in blue air they'll be,
   Singer and sailor.

We, so much older,
   Taller and stronger,
We shall look down on the
   Birdies no longer.

They shall go flying
   With musical speeches
High over head in the
   Tops of the beeches.

In spite of our wisdom
   And sensible talking,
We on our feet must go
   Plodding and walking.

Young Night Thought

All night long and every night,
When my mama puts out the light,
I see the people marching by,
As plain as day, before my eye.

Armies and emperors and kings,
All carrying different kinds of things,
And marching in so grand a way,
You never saw the like by day.

So fine a show was never seen
At the great circus on the green;
For every kind of beast and man
Is marching in that caravan.

At first they move a little slow,
But still the faster on they go,
And still beside them close I keep
Until we reach the town of Sleep.

The Moon

The moon has a face like the clock in the hall;
She shines on thieves on the garden wall,
On streets and fields and harbor quays,
And birdies asleep in the forks of the trees.

The squalling cat and the squeaking mouse,
The howling dog by the door of the house,
The bat that lies in bed at noon,
All love to be out by the light of the moon.

But all of the things that belong to the day
Cuddle to sleep to be out of her way;
And flowers and children close their eyes
Till up in the morning the sun shall arise.

45